Dedic

To the Campbells.
Thank you for your enthusiasm, support, friendship and
for all the fantastic family holidays at Crieff!

Chapter 1

Sophia Slewfoot was an ordinary ten year old girl, but today was not an ordinary day.

Today, for the first time ever, Sophia's best friend Betty Babbington would be coming on holiday with Sophia and her family! Sophia was beyond excited.

It was the end of May and the beginning of the final half term holiday of the year. Spring was in full swing and everywhere Sophia looked the sun was shining, birds were singing and flowers were in full bloom. All of the children and teachers at Sophia's school were feeling happy and re-energised in anticipation of a precious week's holiday before they would have to give one last push of hard work in the final weeks of the academic year.

But none of them, surely, were as happy as Sophia and Betty. Much to the consternation of Sophia's little brother Ted, who was not yet old enough to bring friends away on holiday and would therefore have to be satisfied with the company of just his parents and his Lego on the upcoming trip, Sophia's mum and dad had invited Betty to join them on their half term trip to Scotland. Their thinking was that having Betty accompany the family on a week's break in the estate of a safe and secluded hotel at the gateway to the beautiful Scottish Highlands would afford a good opportunity for Sophia and Betty to start to gain a little independence. Sophia's parents imagined that the girls could safely go off to play tennis together, play the odd round of mini golf and wander around the picturesque grounds and woodlands that surrounded the hotel, before checking back in with them, probably over a drink or a snack, every hour or two. Sophia's friendly and faithful Beagle Toby would, of course, be with them, always taking very seriously his task of protecting and keeping safe his beloved mistress and her funny friend. The girls would, after all, be heading to high school in just over a year's time. It was therefore important that, little by little, the girls should start to build up their confidence in new places and new situations, without their parents being forever right by their side.

(Little did Sophia's parents know, of course, about the many adventures that she and Betty had already had, on many different occasions at different times and in different places, with parents absolutely nowhere on hand! But those are other stories, for another time!)

For those readers who haven't met Sophia Slewfoot before, she was a very happy and outgoing girl. She was short and slight for her age, but she loved dancing and horse-riding and played tennis, netball and football every week. Sophia had crazy, curly blond hair which she studiously tried to tame into a plait or a  ponytail every day, but which inevitably escaped its bobble after approximately five minutes, making her look constantly tousled, no matter how hard she tried! Sophia loved her family and her devoted Tobes, and, along with Betty, she had a great group of girlfriends who were always giggling and gossiping about something. When Sophia felt unsure about something, though, or when she went somewhere new, or met someone for the first time, she could sometimes be quite quiet, even shy. But that probably was why she got on so well with Betty. Betty was tall, strong and a few months older than Sophia. She had long shining, straight blond hair and she was a confident, clever and kindly girl who was pretty-much fearless. Together, one cautious and one carefree, they made a great team.

"So where is it we're going again?" Betty asked as she hauled her suitcase out of her mum's car and up the steps to Sophia's house.

"Oh, hi Bets!" called Sophia, running out of the house to greet her friend and to help her with her luggage. "It's this lovely big old hotel set in acres and acres of grounds in the middle of nowhere in Scotland! I think it's called Crieff Hydro and I bet it's got loads and loads of brilliant stuff for us to do, and loads and loads of exciting places for us to explore..."

"Oooh, yey!" squealed a very excited Betty. She quickly kissed and off-handedly waved goodbye to her mum, who then drove away feeling partly relieved but also, it has to be said, not just a little put out. Betty hadn't given a second thought to the fact that she wouldn't see her mother for a whole week for the first time in her life! "I can't wait!"

"I know!" laughed a very giddy Sophia, "Neither can I!"

"How on earth are we going to put up with these two on the drive all the way up to Crieff?!" wondered Sophia's mum and dad, as they started loading the family's car, roof box and trailer with Betty's and the family's many suitcases, rucksacks, swimming bags, towels, winter coats, waterproofs, spring jackets, smart jackets, wellie boots, flip-flops, trainers, smart shoes, walking boots, walking gear, riding boots, riding gear, bikes, footballs, tennis racquets, tennis balls, golf shoes, golf clubs, dog beds, dog toys, dog blankets, dog towels, dog food, umbrellas, first aid kits, sun creams and all the other gubbins that must be taken on any UK countryside holiday. Of course, the weather could be gloriously hot and sunny one minute, but freezing cold, wet and windy the very next. (You just knew, thought Sophia's parents, that if they didn't pack something, then they would definitely need it; whereas if they packed absolutely everything, then almost none of it would ever get used – it was always the way!)

Finally, after what seemed like an age to the two very excited little girls, but which was actually probably only around twenty minutes at the most, the car was packed, the parents, the children and the dog were in... and they were off!

Chapter 2

"Are we nearly there yet?" chorused Ted, Sophia and Betty only half an hour into what would be at least a four hour drive – longer if the motorway traffic through England was bad (and that was almost inevitable on a Friday at the start of half term).

"Not even close!" laughed Sophia's dad.

"You may as well all just settle into the journey" said Sophia's mum. "Perhaps these will help" and she handed over a travel games console for Ted and the family's tablet (usually used only for schoolwork or a treat, or kept in reserve to maintain the parents' sanity on long drives like this) for Sophia and Betty.

"Why don't you girls do some research into Crieff Hydro Hotel?" suggested Sophia's mum, thinking that might keep the eager pair quiet for at least a little while. "You could find out about all the activities that are on offer at the hotel and perhaps make a plan as to what we can all do while we're there. Have you got a notebook with you to jot down some ideas? Plus, I seem to recall that there might be some interesting history surrounding the building. I'm sure it's been there for well over a hundred years, and old buildings like that usually have a good few stories to tell..."

"Yes, let's do that!" cried Betty. "That will pass some time while we're in the car and it will help us to make the most of our holiday!"

"Of course we've got notebooks with us, Mum!" said Sophia, rolling her eyes. Did her mum not know that Sophia and Betty would never go anywhere unprepared?! In fact, being fans of detective books, adventure stories and whodunnit mysteries, they were both very keen amateur detectives. They spent a lot of their spare time learning about, and honing, their sleuthing skills. In particular, they were well aware that a good detective must always be ready for adventure and action at a moment's notice. Sophia and Betty had therefore each assembled 'go-bags' full of essential kit, including:

- notebooks (elementary, dear reader)
- pens (several, because a detective can't afford for his or her pen to run out just when vital notes need taking)
- a torch (with spare batteries – allowing a torch to die just when you needed it most was, they knew, a real rookie error)
- binoculars

- sunglasses and a selection of hats (for when the need for a swift disguise arises)
- a paperback detective novel (for inspiration and for passing the time on stakeouts)
- a purse containing a few pounds (for emergencies)
- snacks (for energy and because, well, there's always room for snacks)
- a magnifying glass (obviously) and
- one each of a pair of military grade (almost) walkie-talkies, which Sophia had bought with all of her Christmas and birthday money added together.

(The walkie-talkies were primarily for enabling Sophia and Betty to communicate when they were out and about solving mysteries, shadowing suspects and pursuing separate lines of enquiry on active investigations. However they also came in very handy for when the best friends liked to chat to each other from their own homes but were not allowed to borrow and hog their parents' phones.)

In addition, and unknown to anyone but her and Betty (well, and Toby of course, because apart from when she was at school, Tobes never left his lovely mistress' side), Sophia's go-bag also contained something else. Something very, very special and very, very secret.

The very, very special and very, very secret object was Sophia's 'PT machine'. Short for *planisphera temporalabe*[1], the machine resembled, at first glance, an old-fashioned carriage clock that could have held pride of place on a grand Victorian mantelpiece. Shortly after moving into her new (but nearly 300 year old house) in a small village in the North West of England several weeks ago, Sophia had discovered

---

1   *The full, scientific name that Sophia had decided to attribute to the object. Shortly after discovering the object and realising what it could be used for, Sophia had carried out some research into some of the weird and wonderful navigational devices that had been used by travellers and adventurers throughout history – like* **sextants** *which measured the angles between the horizon and the stars to work out latitude, longitude, and therefore location;* **astrolabes**, *which used the sun, stars, the horizon and the meridian for timekeeping, surveying, geography and astrology; and the* **planisphere**, *which was a multi-layered star chart, dating back to the second century, which could be used for calculating the display of visible stars and constellations in the night sky at any time and date.*

Sextant

Astrolabe

Planisphere

the machine in an ancient, rusty safe, which was built into, and camouflaged by, the old, red, crumbling and cobwebby bricks of a secret hidey-hole room that she had found behind a hidden door in an upstairs wall of her home. However, despite appearances, the machine was not just some old clock. Oh no!

The PT machine was made of what must have been real gold, as the object had been locked away for many years, but it was shiny and beautiful and not tarnished at all. The 'clock' face was made of a creamy, shimmering mother-of-pearl, which seemed to glow, even in the tiny, windowless, hidey-hole room in which she had found it. Running around the edge of the face, in Roman numerals fashioned from onyx (a black precious stone), were the numbers 1 to 12, just like you would find on an ordinary clock. That, though, was where the similarities to a clock came to an end.

Running around the circular rim of the object, outside the mother-of-pearl face, and etched into the gold itself, were inscriptions which Sophia had immediately recognised as corresponding to different periods in history. The periods started, at the top of the object, with **Pre-history**, and ran all the way around (in the clockwise direction), through 3000 BC – 476 AD, 477 AD – 1066, 1066 – 1485, 1486 – 1601, 1602 – 1715, 1716 – 1836, 1837 – 1901, 1902 – 1945, to 1946 – 2021. After 1946 – 2021, for the last few degrees of the circle, there was an almost-blank space, marked only with the notation '**?**'.

On the mother-of-pearl face, immediately inside the Roman numerals, at the top, bottom and either side, were the letters **N**, **E**, **S** and **W**, which Sophia now knew stood for north, east, south and west, as on a compass. Then, just inside the compass letters, running clockwise in a circle from the top, were the notations 90°, 60°, 30°, 0°, 30°, 60°; and then 90°, 60°, 30°, 0°, 30° and 60° again. Sophia had learned that those notations referred to latitude and longitude – coordinates by which the location of anywhere on earth can be plotted.

Finally on the mother-of-pearl face of the PT machine, there was a faint, thin line which had been scored delicately across from IX (number 9) on the left-hand side, to III (number 3) on the right, and which therefore effectively divided the face into a top half and a bottom half. A few millimetres above the line, in the centre, was the word **Day**, and a few millimetres below the line was the word **Night**.

Several hands were also affixed to the face. All of the hands were arrow-shaped, so that they could clearly point to a number, letter, notation or word, but otherwise the hands were all different. Some were silvery, some gold, some coppery in colour. Some were shiny, some were dull. Some were plain and some were ornately carved. The various different designs made it easy to see that the different hands each related to a different set of inscriptions or notations. There were a big and a little hand that pointed to the time via the Roman numerals, as on a normal clock. One hand pointed steadfastly to **N** and another spun around to indicate direction via the letters whenever Sophia moved the object, so that, together, they enabled the object to operate as a compass. A quite large hand pointed to a time period and another to **Day** or **Night**. Finally, another pair of hands (again, one big and one little) pointed to the latitude and longitude coordinates.

Soon after finding the fascinating PT machine Sophia had, using her excellent sleuthing and research skills, made the marvellous deduction that the machine was, in fact, a time- and place- travel machine! Sophia had discovered that time and space could be altered and dictated by the moving and setting of the object's various hands. The PT machine enabled a person to go to anywhere in the world, at any point throughout history, and to have amazing adventures before returning home safely, with time, in the real life present day, having stood still all the while.

Sophia and Betty had used the PT machine to go on many exciting expeditions through time and throughout the world. They had even had a number of adventures solving some of history's greatest mysteries[2]. The girls had therefore, on a number of occasions now, actually been more brave, confident and independent than their parents would ever have guessed in their wildest dreams (or, more likely, in their wildest nightmares)!

---

2   *Those are, of course, the other stories that were mentioned earlier!*

In any event, thrilled to have an opportunity to dive into their go-bags so early into the holiday, and to have an excuse to start doing research and making notes (both of which are extremely enjoyable pastimes for ten year old girls everywhere) Sophia and Betty grabbed their notebooks and pens, and typed "Crieff Hydro Hotel" into the search engine on their tablet.

Chapter 3

Sophia's mum had been right. There was so much to learn about what Crieff Hydro had to offer, and also about its fascinating history, that the girls were engrossed in their research, note-taking and holiday-planning for almost all of the journey up to the beautiful, rugged and remote Scottish Highlands.

Betty took charge of making notes of some of the activities that she, Sophia, Ted and Sophia's parents might like to do during their stay at Crieff Hydro:

- Glen's Adventure Park
  - Peddle carts
  - Swings
  - Zip wires
  - Slides
  - Spiders web climbing
  - Hide and seek
  - Basecamp café
- Action Glen
  - Treetop adventure
  - Segways

- Quad bikes
- Mini 4x4 off-road driving for the kids
- Archery
- Woodland combat
- Air rifles
- Mountain biking — ugh we didn't need to bring all our own bikes!
- Tourer cycling
- Crazy golf
- The grounds
  - Hiking up the Knock
  - Lady Mary's river walk (note, further research needed: who is/was Lady Mary?)
  - Walking round the grounds
  - Walking the woodland trails
  - Horse riding lessons
  - Horse riding hacks
  - Bouncy castle
  - Lawn games
  - Children's entertainer/magician
- The loch
  - Paddle boarding
  - Cold water swimming
  - The Bunker
  - Golf simulator

- Juke box karaoke
- Pool
- Game zone
- Indoor sports
- Glen's Den
  - Virtual Reality machine
  - X-box
  - Indoor air ice hockey, table football, pool and arcade machines
- Golf
- Tennis
- 5-a-side football
- Squash
- Badminton
- Basketball
- Spa
  - Pool
  - Adults only Victorian Baths (query: what will the parents do with Ted?)
  - Gym
  - Yoga
  - Sauna, steam, spa baths
- Eateries
  - The Meikle

- The Tiffin Tearoom at The Winter Garden
- The Terrace
- The Hub
- Entertainment
  - Cinema
  - Big Country indoor childcare centre (note: oh, that's what the parents will do with Ted!)
  - Other ad-hoc entertainment options on offer — multi-sports, lawn games, treasure hunts, Lego sessions, craft sessions, bowling green, and more!

When Betty had finished and shared her notes, the only problems that the happy holiday party could anticipate were either that a week's stay would not give them long enough to try out all the activities, or that they would go home so exhausted that they would immediately feel the need for another break away!

Sophia took charge of making notes about some of the interesting historical background to the current Crieff Hydro Hotel:

● 1867 – a Dr Thomas Meikle was inspired, following his stay at a therapeutic retreat in Austria which offered guests rejuvenation and healing, to open his own such institution. Dr Meikle's regime would be based on drinking large amounts of water, exercise, fresh mountain air, water treatments and eating only small portions of simple, even coarse, country food

Dr Thomas Meikle

Outdoor Exercise

● 1868 – Crieff Hydropathic Establishment was opened, offering clean eating, prayers and religious instruction, brisk outdoor exercise, somewhat questionable (!) hydropathic/water treatments (think, ice-cold dips on strict nurses' orders), and absolutely no alcohol anywhere on site

Crieff Hydropathic Establishment

"What?!" cried Sophia's mum, with a look of what could only be described as sheer panic on her face, when Sophia read out this

24

particular part of her notes.

"Don't worry!" laughed her dad. "That was way back when – it's not like that now! There are bars, cafés and restaurants, serving excellent food and drink of all kinds, throughout Crieff Hydro nowadays! Honestly, I promise, love. It was one of the first things I checked before booking!"

Ferntower House

● 1939 – 1945 During the Second World War, Polish forces were billeted in Ferntower House, on the hotel estate, as part of the Allied efforts against Nazi Germany

● 1939 – 1945 Polish soldiers report 'hauntings' of Ferntower House by a mysterious 'White lady'

● Ferntower House was eventually abandoned and it deteriorated over time. It was demolished in 1963

● 2018 – Crieff Hydro celebrated its 150th birthday with hundreds of guests and hotel friends and family members enjoying food, drink, lawn games, stalls, live music and more!

Reading back through Sophia's notes together, she and Betty exchanged a knowing glance and experienced an electrifying thrill – there was a history mystery here for them to solve! Maybe even a real life ghost story! Who was the Crieff Hydro White Lady? Where did she come from? *When* did she come from? Did she still roam the hotel? Was she good or was she evil? What was her story, and was it a happy one, or was it sad?

Sophia and Betty were determined, as soon as they got chance (in between all the other exciting activities and entertainments, of course!), to use Sophia's precious PT machine to find out...

Chapter 4

A few hours later, after what did turn out to be a bit of a slog through half term Friday traffic up the motorway from Cheshire, past the Lake District and into Scotland, Sophia, Betty, Sophia's parents, Toby and a very tired Ted pulled into the grounds of Crieff Hydro. In the soft light of the late evening sunset, the majesty and beauty of the huge, imposing hotel took their breath away.

Crieff Hydro

Sophia and Betty felt their skin prickle and the hairs on the back of their necks stand on end – not with fear or trepidation at all, but with excitement for the holiday that lay ahead; with delight at the thought of all the fun they would have at the 'Action Glen' adventure park and exploring the extensive estate; and with anticipation of the amateur sleuthing, the mystery solving and even the ghost hunting, that they knew the coming week would entail.

Despite the fact that the long journey had started to lull Ted and even, to some extent, the two girls almost into a slightly slumbering state, once they were inside the hotel, the hustle and bustle of the busy reception soon had the children feeling energised again, and raring to go!

Ted barely had time to play on the Virtual Reality game machine that was housed in one corner of the lofty, light-filled lobby, before the family were checked-in and being welcomed by the hotel manager. The next minute they were guided past richly decorated corridors which wound into the far reaches of the big, old building, and through an enormous nineteenth century dance hall, into the elegant conservatory café known as The Tiffin Tearoom, in the spectacular, circular, glass-built, light-filled Winter Garden.

Sophia and Betty couldn't wait to start exploring the hotel and delving in to all the activities, secrets and surprises they knew it would have to offer. However, they were soon too busy tucking into an absolutely delicious late tea of sandwiches, crisps, fruit, cake and fizzy pop to feel too impatient.

As the children ate and drank to their hearts' content (and to their parents', as all three children were calm, quiet and still for once!), they listened carefully to the hotel manager as he explained the timetable of additional events that would be taking place the next day: a multi-sports morning, a Lego competition (just the thing for Ted!), and a craft club to name but a few! When the manager mentioned that there would be a treasure hunt around the hotel and its grounds, with the first clue being released in the dance hall just after lunchtime, Sophia and Betty nodded happily to each other. That would be the perfect way to kick off their explorations!

A short while later, stuffed full of tasty teatime treats, and feeling warm, comfy and cosy in their luxurious but homely hotel room (which adjoined Sophia's parents' and Ted's room via a cool connecting door), the girls whispered gleefully to each other long into the first, and very novel, night of their holiday.

Amongst all sorts of other things (such as, favourite song from 'The Greatest Showman'; favourite pony at their riding school; favourite character from 'High School Musical'; would you rather: ballet or tap, football or netball, Famous Five or Secret Seven; etc), the girls chatted about their plans for the next day, as well as the steps they would take to solve the mystery of the White Lady. As the night drew to a close, with Toby curled up in his bed alongside Sophia's, snug as a bug in a rug having a hug, and snoring softly, the girls finally drifted off contentedly into a peaceful, deep and dream-filled sleep.

Chapter 5

Bright and early the next morning, feeling refreshed and ready to go after a lovely (if not particularly long) sleep, Sophia and Betty made their way, with Sophia's family, to the grand Meikle restaurant – named after Crieff Hydro's founder and ancestor of the current owners, Dr Thomas Meikle.

From the reading that she had done about the rather scant, simple country food that was on offer when the Hydropathic Establishment first opened, Sophia couldn't help but wonder what the strict and abstemious doctor would have made of the staggering spread that was a Crieff Hydro breakfast today! Sophia and Betty simply couldn't get over the mountains of bacon, sausages, eggs (scrambled, fried, poached, boiled, hard-boiled), beans, mushrooms, tomatoes, hash browns, haggis, Scotch pancakes, rolls, toast, jams, marmalades, peanut butter, marmite, chocolate spread, croissants, pastries, cereals of every kind (including all the chocolatey and sugary ones that were usually only allowed as an extra-special treat), porridge, ham, cheese, fruit, yogurts and more, not to mention an array of every kind of hot and cold drink you could ever imagine. Sophia and Betty might not be able to believe the scale, quality and variety of the breakfast on offer, but that certainly didn't stop them from getting stuck in! After a very pleasant half an hour or so, during which they and Ted consumed probably more food in just one breakfast than they would usually consume in a good couple of days, the girls were feeling more than sufficiently fortified for their holiday activities and adventures to begin!

"Sophs" said Betty, "we've got around an hour before the start of the multi-sports morning, plus I need to let my breakfast go down before I attempt anything too physically demanding or I'll be sick! Shall we go and check out the cinema, the pool area and the Bunker indoor entertainment area, in case we want to do any of those things later on today?

"Oh yes, that is a good idea" said Sophia, who was actually feeling fit to burst after her breakfast extravaganza. "Mum, Dad, will that be ok? Bets and I will be able to find our way around, no problem, as all the different areas in the hotel are so well signposted, plus there are staff members everywhere. We will be able to meet up with you an hour from now on the sports field just next to the Victorian Garden. That's where the multi-sports morning is taking place, and I know that Ted will want to join in with that too."

"Yes, that will be fine" smiled Sophia's mum. "We'll give Toby a quick walk and take Ted along to have a look at the Big Country indoor childcare centre in case he fancies having a quick play, then we'll meet you on the sports field as you suggest."

"Great, thanks!" chorused Sophia and Betty, already racing off. "See you in a bit!"

After looking in on the hotel's amazing cinema suite (where tonight's showing would be a cartoon superhero film that Ted would love) and having a quick blast on the air ice hockey and table football games at the Bunker, the girls made their way to the pool and spa area of the hotel.

Sophia and Betty laughed and danced along corridor after corridor together, turning first one way and then another. They skipped past happy couples, noisy families and lots of busy staff members. Before long they turned to follow a sign that directed the girls to take a flight of stairs down, round a corner, down, and round and down again, until they reached what must surely be the very bottom of the building.

All of a sudden the happy hubbub of the busy

hotel made way for the calm, quiet, almost serene, atmosphere of the spa. Guests wandered around, seemingly aimlessly, in fluffy white dressing gowns and slippers. Softly smiling staff members passed noiselessly in and out of treatment rooms. The temperature had undoubtedly risen several degrees above what it had been before the girls had descended the several flights of stairs, and gentle pan pipe music floated from hidden speakers. Sophia and Betty both felt suddenly subdued.

"Gosh Sophs" murmured Betty in a hushed tone that Sophia didn't think she had ever heard Betty use before. "This is all very nice and restful, and I'm sure that your mum and dad would love it down here if they could get Ted booked into the childcare centre at some point this week, but I'm not really sure it's for me. What with that massive breakfast and now all this hypnotic, floaty, flutey music, I feel like I'm in danger of falling asleep! I don't think we're in quite the right area for the kids' leisure pool."

"Hmm, you might be right" whispered Sophia. "There seemed to be so many twists and turns as we made our way down here, we must have missed a sign for the leisure pool and made our way to the spa treatment area instead. Wait a minute, though, what's that? Is that the pool do you think?"

A very relaxed-looking lady in a bathrobe, with her hair wrapped in a towel turban, had come through a doorway just ahead of them, and Sophia had glimpsed a shimmer of glistening aquamarine. The intoxicating scent of chlorine mixed with essential oils of eucalyptus, mint and lavender followed the lady, and so Sophia and Betty thought that they must have happened upon the pool area after all.

As they pushed open the heavy door, though, the two girls remembered that Crieff Hydro had not only a big leisure pool where children and families could swim and play, but that it also had an adults-only pool, known as the Victorian Baths. That, surely, was where Sophia and Betty found themselves now.

The beautiful, shimmering pool before them was completely empty, as were the several sumptuous lounge-beds that were dotted here and there around the poolside. As soon as the door had swung silently shut behind them, an all-but absolute silence fell over the room. The two girls found themselves soundlessly admiring the soft-lit haven, which was tastefully tiled in the distinct, sophisticated,

Victorian spa style.

Just as Sophia was about to turn to Betty and suggest that they re-trace their steps to try to find the family pool, she stopped short. Sophia suddenly stood frozen still, as the strangest sensation she had ever experienced – stranger, even, than the jolt, thwack and flash that accompanied Sophia's journeys through time and space each time she used the miraculous PT machine – stole fleetingly, but unmistakeably, over her entire body.

It was as if all of the significant heat and humidity of the spa area had been sucked away in a single second. A deep, bone-chilling cold, more freezing than the darkest, iciest, winter night that Sophia had ever known, wormed its way right through her. From her front to her back, from her toes to the tip of her head, and then, for an instant only – an absolutely miniscule measure of time, but one that would stay with her in her thoughts and her dreams for evermore – it was as if a small, razor sharp icicle had pierced, and passed right through, her heart.

At exactly the same moment that Sophia froze, Betty swung her head around so fast, to stare incredulously in Sophia's direction, that she actually seemed to snap a muscle in her neck. Not that Betty felt a thing, though. Oh no. She was too busy stuttering, stammering and pointing at what she would later describe (once she had recovered from the shock and regained her power of speech, that is) as a spectral white shape. It had appeared out of nowhere and seemed to glide, swiftly and soundlessly, through the specific spot on which Sophia was standing – as if actually through Sophia herself! Then, almost immediately, it disappeared again, vanishing into thin air.

"W-w-what, w-what, on earth was that?!" shrieked Sophia as soon as the funny, freezing, stifling, slicing sensation had passed.

"I, I, um, I, uh... I don't know" stuttered Betty, faltering and holding up her hands in a gesture of bewilderment.

That was something Sophia had never seen before, and she didn't like it. This was her best friend Betty Babbington, who always had the answers – to everything, anything! If Betty didn't know what she had seen, what Sophia had experienced, what was going on, then the girls were potentially very much out of their depth. Without Betty being able to offer an explanation for the strange and unsettling events of the last few seconds or minutes (Sophia had lost all track of time and all sense of reality), Sophia suddenly felt frightened, nervous, vulnerable even.

Then, with a flash of inspiration of which any amateur sleuth would be proud, Sophia remembered the research that she had done during the long car journey up to Crieff...

"Oh my goodness!" cried Sophia, as a terrifying, but also a fascinating, idea dawned on her. "Bets! I think I know what that might have been! I think, oh gosh, I actually really do think... Betty, we may have just encountered the g-g-ghost! C-c-rieff Hydro's White Lady!"

Chapter 6

Not wanting to remain in the Victorian Baths even a millisecond longer, Sophia and Betty instinctively grabbed each other by the hand and ran, pell mell, out of the door through which they had come. The girls ducked past several ladies who, if they hadn't been blissed-out and in a state of extreme relaxation following the massages, facials, hot stone treatments, reflexology and Prosecco that they had just enjoyed, would surely have been alarmed at the sight of two young girls apparently fleeing the spa area as if for their lives.

Not pausing to read any of the signposts which were designed to direct guests effortlessly and efficiently around the hotel, Sophia and Betty rushed, as quickly as they could, up several flights of stairs. They ran along a number of richly carpeted corridors and dashed through the main dance hall, before bursting out into the welcome, reassuringly normal, bright, fresh sunshine of the late May mid-morning. Only then did they stop to gather their thoughts and to catch their breath.

"Sophs," began Betty, "I think we need to take a break from exploring for a while. I, I never thought I'd say this, but I think I fancy a bit of time off from adventure and mystery-solving and g-g-ghost stories".

"Of course Bets" agreed Sophia. "I feel exactly the same. I suppose I am curious about what I just felt and what you just saw, but I'm definitely not in the mood just now for any more shocks or scary surprises."

"Come on then" said Betty, taking a rousing deep breath and giving herself a shake. "I'd say that what we need is a morning full of fun and games with your mum, dad and Ted in this lovely weather in these gorgeous grounds! Let's head over to the sports field – we're just in time for the multi-sports morning!"

"Yey!" laughed Sophia. "Let the games begin!"

And, just like that, the two bright girls bounced straight back into their normal, cheery, happy-go-lucky selves. In no time at all they and Ted were running, jumping, relaying, hurdling and hoola-ing round Crieff Hydro's immaculately-kept sports field without a care in the world, while Sophia's mum and dad looked on contentedly (and enjoyed a rather special, strong, rich, frothy, Italian coffee). Perfect!

Chapter 7

Although they would never have imagined, after consuming a breakfast on the scale that they had done that morning, that they would ever feel hungry enough for lunch, Sophia and Betty surprised themselves by agreeing whole-heartedly that they would indeed enjoy a quick burger and chips at the Hub café, when Sophia's parents suggested it.

The happy party settled around a table outside the relaxed sports café. While they waited for their lunch to be brought to them, Sophia's dad and Ted watched sport on the Hub's massive TV; Sophia's mum grabbed the opportunity to read a few pages of her book; Toby curled up for a quick nap at Sophia's feet (the exertion of his morning walk, plus the excitement of the multi-sports morning – and his frustration and not being allowed off his lead to join in! – had worn him out); and Sophia and Betty turned their attention, once again, to their unsettling experience of earlier that morning.

"How do you feel now about what happened this morning, Bets?" asked Sophia. "Are you still feeling a bit shaken and reluctant to find out more, or are you starting to feel excited again by the prospect of the mystery of Crieff Hydro's White Lady?"

"Actually," began Betty "I'm not really feeling frightened about what happened this morning at all anymore. I know that we were both very much taken aback at the time by what I think must have been our supernatural encounter, but the more I think about it, the more I believe that there's actually nothing for us to be scared of."

"What do you mean, Bets?" asked Sophia. "If you really do think that we encountered the ghost of the White Lady, why don't you think there's anything for us to fear?"

"Well," explained Betty "it's like this. I genuinely believe that I actually saw the ghost of the White Lady. I definitely saw a white, spectral shape. The more I think about it, the more I can see in my mind's eye that it almost certainly was the figure of a lady dressed in flowing clothes – the type that would have been in fashion a couple of hundred years ago. I also genuinely believe that you felt the ghost of the White Lady, because I saw her walk right through where you were standing, so right through you! However, despite what we saw and felt, absolutely no harm came to us at all. The White Lady didn't seem angry or scary or cross or evil or malevolent in any way. She was, well, she was, just, there. And another thing, if the White Lady was a scary or an evil ghost, I can't imagine that the family that owns this hotel can have managed to repeatedly receive hundreds of thousands of happy holiday guests here for over 150 years, with absolutely no sinister feelings or horrible happenings ever being reported. I don't think that anything like that was revealed by any of the research that you did into the history of the hotel, was it? So, I think that the White Lady must be a friendly, or at the very least a harmless, ghost. So, all in all, I'm simply not scared anymore. How about you?"

"I'm really pleased that you've said that!" smiled Sophia. This was the Betty that she knew and loved, fully back to her usual confident and clever self! "I feel exactly the same as you and I'm not at all worried about the White Lady. I don't think I'd even be scared if I crossed paths with her again or if I saw her like you did. No, in fact, I think I feel more intrigued, more curious now than ever to find out about and solve the mystery of the White Lady."

"Right then," determined Betty. "It's agreed. We'll

scope out this whole place this afternoon under the guise of completing the treasure hunt, and then we'll formulate a plan as to how exactly we solve Crieff Hydro's very own 'history's mystery'!"

Chapter 8

After a delicious lunch of one of the largest, sweetest, juiciest, cheesiest burgers that Sophia and Betty had ever eaten, the two girls and the intrepid Tobes made their way to the beautiful, majestic dance hall, known as the Ballroom, where the treasure hunt was about to begin.

While they were waiting for the treasure hunt, the two girls, who both enjoyed going to an after-school Street Dance club each week and had been to ballet classes when they were younger, gazed around the Ballroom with admiration and wonder. The Crieff Hydro website had explained that the stunning space was still used for ceilidhs and weddings and gala dinners and graduation balls today. In the girls' imagination, however, the room was twinkling with the lights from nineteenth century chandeliers and filled with the clinking of glasses and the drumming of dancing heels on the polished wooden floor. The girls could almost hear the classical music and the swish of silk gowns from balls and formal dances and parties and elegant gatherings from years and years and years gone by.

Almost reluctantly, the girls were pulled from their reveries of bygone revelries when one of the hotel's leisure managers suddenly called all the treasure hunters to attention, and released the first clue!

Now, for the sake of those readers who might visit Crieff Hydro one day and might endeavour to complete one of the tremendous treasure hunts that are hosted from time to time, the clues that Sophia and Betty were given and, of course, the solutions that these two excellent, albeit amateur, detectives quickly devised, will not be revealed. However, suffice to say that, over the course of the afternoon, Sophia and Betty solved clue after clue after clue. In doing so, they followed a trail that took them all over the hotel, its extensive grounds, and even through some of the woodland, riverside and countryside that comprised this magnificent estate.

As any self-respecting amateur sleuth would, Sophia and Betty had taken their go-bags with them while they were out and about treasure-hunting, and it turned out that they were very glad indeed that they had done so. Not only did the girls stop to enjoy a couple of the snacks that they always kept in their go-bags (despite their mega breakfast and mega burgers – they were on holiday after all), but also there were several opportunities during the treasure hunt for copious, important note-taking.

Of particular interest in relation to the telling of this story, were the notes that the girls made when their clue-solving led them to the Action Glen area – in particular a section of the golf course across which Sophia and Betty had to walk to discover clue number 9; a section of the spectacular Lady Mary's Walk, alongside the beautiful River Earn; and one of the corridors on the lowermost level of the hotel. On each of those occasions the girls made the specific note:

"Experienced a temporary but distinct drop in temperature at this location, accompanied by a sudden and short lived draught or blast of cold air. Strange, on an otherwise warm and still late May afternoon."

On each of those occasions, however, the two girls were simply too busy solving and following treasure hunt clues, enjoying their stunning surroundings and relishing the opportunity to make concise and accurate notes in their go-bag notebooks, to notice the insubstantial flash of ghostly white that quietly passed them by, time after time after time...

Chapter 9

Although Sophia and Betty had decided that they were not at all scared by (and in fact they were fascinated by, and determined to explain) the mystery of the Crieff Hydro White Lady, their scheme to devise a plan for actually solving the enigma was inevitably put on hold for the next couple of days. Having completed the treasure hunt and actually seen first-hand a lot of the activities that the hotel had to offer, the girls were simply so keen to have a go at the zip wires, Segways, jumping pillows, quad bikes, mini 4x4s, archery and woodland combat at Action Glen, that they had to take a couple of days' break from amateur sleuthing.

Then, feeling very tired but very happy one evening a few days later, while Sophia's mum and dad enjoyed a drink in the Terrace restaurant and watched over Ted as he jumped around on the bouncy castle and challenged another little boy to a game of outdoor chess (played by very unconventional and not entirely recognisable rules), Sophia and Betty turned their attention once more to the mystery of the Crieff Hydro White Lady.

"So, Sophs," said Betty. "We've only got a few days of the holiday left. What do you think should be our plan of action for finding out more about this White Lady ghost?"

"I've been thinking about that Bets" said Sophia. "To some extent we know what to do with the PT machine. I mean, on the one hand it's pretty obvious that we should simply set the latitude and longitude co-ordinates to just here, at the Crieff Hydro Estate, to discover the origins of the White Lady ghost. On the other hand, though, we've currently got no idea as to *when* in history we should try to visit to attempt to get to the bottom of things. So, I think that we need to use our 'little grey cells'[3] a bit more, and perhaps do some more research, to give ourselves a better idea of what exactly we are looking for and *when*. Once we know that, we can set the PT machine to a suitable time and date, and we can then take a

---

3   *Agatha Christie's famous eccentric Belgian detective Hercule Poirot, who was a great favourite of Sophia and Betty, often refers to using his 'little grey cells' – meaning exercising brain power and the value of simple, careful thought – when it comes to the solving of mysteries.*

trip to observe whoever the White Lady was when she was alive!"

"Elementary, my dear Sophia," pronounced Betty. "We have a plan!"

Chapter 10

The next morning (after yet another hearty breakfast!) Sophia, Betty and Toby had a full couple of hours to themselves while Sophia's mum and dad did indeed head down to the spa for some serious relaxation and Ted went to Big Country to play with a number of friends that he had made during the family's stay in Crieff Hydro. After joining in the multi-sports morning, playing in an under 8s 5-a-side football tournament, playing outdoor chess (of sorts) and spending literally hours on the bouncy castle in front of the Terrace restaurant, Ted had made quite a tight-knit group of friends. It turned out that pretty-much every other little boy that Ted had met also liked superheroes, Lego, football and tearing around like there was no tomorrow – who'd have thought it?!

Sophia and Betty grabbed their go-bags and tablet and decided to take Toby for a nice walk to a peaceful spot where they could rest up, have a drink and a snack (of course), and carry out some more research into the possible origins of the Crieff Hydro White Lady.

"How about we go up The Knock, Sophs?" suggested Betty. "It's supposed to be great hike through the woods above and behind the hotel, with really spectacular views all around when you reach the top. I'm sure that we and Tobes could do with really stretching our legs, plus we should be able to find somewhere nice and quiet where we can do our research without being disturbed."

"Oh yes, that sounds perfect!" agreed Sophia. And so they were off!

After a very pleasant, if quite strenuous, ramble along winding, climbing, shady trails through the rich, ancient woodland behind Crieff Hydro, Sophia and Betty reached the summit of the Knock.

On breaking through the dense cover of lush trees, the girls were met by a sight that was breathtaking indeed. The views from the top of the Knock seemed to roll on forever. The land all around was every shade of green, gold, red, orange and brown, with bright flashes of purple on the horizon where soft heather and Scottish thistles carpeted the land. The boundary between the land and the overarching, ever-changing sky was blurred by a lazy summer haze and by misty, ephemeral clouds. The girls stood, transfixed, as the dramatic Highland scenery extended beyond them, untouched and immaculate, as far as the eye could see.

"Gosh!" breathed Sophia gently.

"Wow!" gushed Betty. "I think it's the most beautiful place I have ever been. Thank you so much for inviting me on this trip, Sophia."

"You're very welcome Bets!" laughed Sophia. "Without you here I doubt I'd ever have had the courage to continue investigating the mystery of the White Lady after our encounter the other day! So, shall we sit here awhile, in this gorgeous, tranquil spot, and work on putting the next stage of our plan into action?"

"Yes, definitely" said Betty. "Now, before we start any further research to follow on from the historical information that you have already discovered, I seem to remember that there was a question outstanding from some of the research that I was doing that's been niggling at me a bit..." Betty was flipping back through her notebook and looking over the information that she had jotted down during their car journey on the way up to Crieff. "Yes, that's it, here it is!" she remarked suddenly. Betty showed an extract from her activities research to Sophia:

● The grounds
  – Hiking up the Knock
  – Lady Mary's river walk (note, further research needed: who is/was Lady Mary?)
  – Walking round the grounds

"Of course!" cried Sophia. "Good thinking Bets! If the ghost is known as the White Lady and there's an unexplained reference to a Lady Mary on the estate, that's a great place to start!"

So, energised with the fresh enthusiasm for the case that comes with any possible new lead, our two sleuths opened up their tablet – incongruous though that was in the pure, natural and age-old beauty of their surroundings – and tapped "Lady Mary, Crieff" into the search engine.

Chapter 11

In the idyllic setting of the top of the Knock, high above the hotel and looking out into the vast and rugged beauty of the Scottish Highlands, Sophia Slewfoot and Betty Babbington started to research, in earnest, the mystery of Crieff Hydro's ghost, the White Lady.

Here is a copy of the notes that Sophia and Betty made in their detective's notebook, after typing into their tablet's search engine the phrase "Lady Mary, Crieff":

- The 'Lady Mary' of Lady Mary's Walk, Crieff, is Lady Mary Murray, daughter to Sir Patrick Murray (1771–1837). (Sir Patrick was also known sometimes as Sir Peter Murray.) He was the Laird (Lord) of Ochtertyre and a judge and statesman.

- Sir Patrick Murray and his family lived at Ferntower House. Sir Patrick created 'Lady Mary's Walk, a picturesque path along the River Earn that was favoured by his daughter Mary, sometime around 1814–15.

- Lady Mary married James Bonar of Kimmerghame (1795 – 1867) on 11 September 1839 and she died on 4 July 1886.

- Sir Patrick/Peter Murray was friendly with famous Regency composer/band leader Nathaniel Gow (1763 – 1831).

- Nathaniel Gow composed a tune entitled 'Lady Mary Murray'.

- Ferntower House was situated on the Crieff Hydro estate until it became so dilapidated and ravaged by the passage of time that it was ultimately demolished in 1963. Ferntower House stood on ground which now forms part of the hotel's golf course.

"What do you make of all that Bets?" asked Sophia. "I think that we've found our Lady Mary, and that she might well be a contender for being the 'White Lady', but she must have lived for many, many years in the nineteenth century. She was old enough to have a favourite walk by 1815 and she lived until 1886. How on earth do we decide which date we want to visit..." (at this point, even though there probably wasn't another soul to be found for at least a mile around in any and every direction) Sophia lowered her voice to a whisper "...using the PT machine?"

"Hmm," said Betty thoughtfully. "I suppose it doesn't matter if we don't manage to zoom off, immediately on our first attempt, to the exact moment in history that will solve this mystery. If we try a particular date and it doesn't really shed any light, then surely we can just try and try again? After all, we've got a few days of the holiday still left; and anyway, isn't it the case that time in the real life here and now stands still whenever we are time- and place-travelling with the PT machine?"

"Ye-es, that is strictly correct" agreed Sophia slowly, "but it is quite a shock to the system when you travel using the PT machine, so it's probably sensible for us not to do it more than we really, really need to."

"Oh, ok, I understand" said Betty. "Then, yes, I agree, we do have a bit of a problem. We've narrowed our field of investigation to the Crieff Hydro estate in terms of the *where*, but we're still looking at most of the nineteenth century in terms of the *when*."

"Wait a minute!" cried Sophia excitedly all of a sudden. "I think I might have an idea. Didn't we learn from the outset that there were several reports of sightings of the White Lady when the old Ferntower House was occupied by Allied Polish forces during World War Two? What if we initially set the time machine to, say, 1944, when we know that Polish soldiers were living in Ferntower House? We could perhaps manage to witness a haunting ourselves, or we can listen in to the soldiers' reports first-hand. Either way, I think that we should try to discover the approximate age of the White Lady. If we can discover that the ghost is a young lady, then we can set the PT machine to the early 1800s sometime; if we learn that the ghost is an older lady, then we can set the machine to later in the nineteenth century, when Lady Mary Murray would have been an older lady herself?"

"That definitely sounds to me like the best idea that we have got" stated Betty decisively. "Yes – let's do just that!"

Just at that moment, however, Toby, who had been dozing peacefully, snuggled in Sophia's lap all the time that the girls had been carrying out their research, making their notes and formulating the next steps in their mystery-solving adventure, jumped up. With his ears standing right up and his hind legs taught, Toby alerted the girls to the presence of a young family, happily puffing and panting their way up to the top of the Knock. On arriving at the summit, the family began to unpack a tasty-looking picnic just a few feet away from where Sophia, Betty and Toby had been sitting.

"Mmmm" murmured Sophia and Betty in chorus. "All of a sudden a nice lunch seems like a very good idea!"

And with that, the two girls and their protective pooch made their way quickly and carefully back down the hill, through the woods, and in to the hotel. The girls met Sophia's mum and dad (both of whom were more relaxed and happy, after their spa treatments, than Sophia thought she had ever seen them before) and Ted, just outside the Big Country childcare centre.

"Where shall we go for lunch today, kids?" asked Sophia's dad. "We've been to the Hub, the Terrace, the Winter Garden tea room and the Miekle several times already. I think I fancy something new today. How about we try out the estate's local pub for a change? I think it's called the Murray Park."

Sophia and Betty exchanged a knowing glance and a happy smile with each other. "The 'Murray' Park, Dad?" laughed Sophia. "That sounds perfect – let's go!"

Chapter 12

Having agreed upon a strategy to really put their mystery-solving investigation into action, and having been enthused and excited by what the girls felt sure were some really good leads to help them learn the story of the White Lady, the reader might be surprised to learn that Sophia and Betty actually didn't manage to action their plan for another couple of days. Unknown to the girls, Sophia's parents had booked a fantastically enjoyable horse-riding hack for the girls, which took them around some of the wooded and waterside paths around the estate that they had not yet otherwise explored. The happy holiday party also spent a really memorable day swimming, paddle-boarding and picnicking at the loch, which was just a short way down the glen from the hotel.

So, the minute the girls found themselves with an hour or so of free time one evening, they quickly scampered off, apparently on the pretence of taking Toby for a good, long walk, but actually intending to travel, though history, back to 1944, when Ferntower House had stood on what is now Crieff Hydro Hotel's golf course.

The girls had eaten a light, early tea with Sophia's mum, dad and Ted before Sophia's parents took Ted to watch a magic show with the one of the hotel's excellent children's entertainers. It was therefore around 7 pm on a warm, dry, late spring evening, by the time the girls found a secluded spot on the almost-empty golf course from which they could carry out their plan.

It was a beautiful evening and a serene setting. The clear sky, somewhere between daylight and twilight, was just starting to turn pink and pale purple in places, but there would be no sign of darkness creeping in for several hours yet. It was nearly the longest day of the year, after all. The birds were singing and the air all around was buzzing with the incessant wings of a thousand busy insects. It really was not the stereotypical scene for a ghost hunt.

However, ducking down out of sight in a bunker, just in case any straggling golfers were still finishing their round, Sophia and Betty huddled together and carefully pulled out of Sophia's go-bag the amazing, the fantastical, the magical PT machine. Despite the atypical setting, ghost-hunting was exactly what Sophia and Betty proposed to do!

The girls had already pre-set the PT machine's latitude and longitude coordinates hands to 56.3797° **N** and 3.8378° **W**, which they knew to represent the location of the Crieff Hydro estate. They had also set the time to 11 o'clock (**Night**) on the assumption that later into the night might be a more likely time to experience a haunting. Now that they were actually ready to 'go' (a strangely insufficient phrase to describe the fact that they would be travelling through time, yes; but that they would not actually be moving anywhere else in terms of location!), Sophia and Betty only needed to set the PT machine's time period hand to 1944 and to hold on to the PT machine, to each other, and to Tobes, as tightly as they possibly could, and then...

All of a sudden, with a w h o o s h k a z z a m f l a s h z i n g w o w !!!, the girls and the faithful Tobes (who was, by now, getting somewhat used to travelling PT machine-style, even if he was not yet what you could describe as keen on the experience) Sophia and Betty felt an electrifying jolt through their bodies. Both of the girls experienced a punch-like thwack in their tummy and their chest, as if all of their breath had been sucked from them for several seconds. They squeezed their eyes tight shut to protect them from the blinding glare of a flashing light that was brighter and more dazzling than anything they had ever seen before. And then, almost immediately, all was quiet and calm, and Sophia, Betty and Toby felt absolutely like themselves again.

The girls opened their eyes. They were pleased as punch to see that they were standing in the same picturesque landscape which, in the real life here and now they knew was dotted about with flags, holes and amateur/holidaying golfers; but which was, in the now of a late night sometime in 1944, clearly part of the extended grounds of the residence known as Ferntower House.

Before doing anything at all, however, before even taking a single step, Sophia unbuckled the belt from her jeans and carefully looped it through the handle at the top of the PT machine. She also looped Toby's lead through her belt hooks and grabbed Betty's hand and held onto it, tight.

"Bets," explained Sophia, "I know that this is all a bit cumbersome, but you know that we must all absolutely remain attached to each other, and therefore to the PT machine, *at all times*. You must not let go of my hand *at any point, even for a second* while we are time-travelling. Whatever happens while we are on any history's mystery adventure, we and the PT machine must not, on any account, become separated. The PT machine is our only means of getting home to the real life present day, and back to the safety of my mum and dad and the hotel. If we don't hold on to the PT machine, we risk never being able to get back home, and being lost in time forever. So please, whatever you do, don't let go!"

"I know, I understand Sophs, don't worry" said Betty. And with that, the little close-knit group (close-knit in more ways than one!) began to make its way, warily, slowly and somewhat clumsily, through the darkening night, across the Ferntower grounds, towards the house itself.

Chapter 13

Sophia, Betty and Toby were really on a history's mystery-solving mission now. They had worked out that the 'Lady Mary' of Lady Mary's Walk was probably the daughter of the wealthy, influential Laird Murray who had lived at Ferntower House in the 1700s and 1800s. They had deduced that Lady Mary Murray was a contender for Crieff Hydro Hotel's White Lady ghost, but they wanted to make sure. They also wanted to understand the White Lady's story. Why did she haunt Crieff Hydro? Was she a harmless ghost or a malevolent one? Was her story a happy one or was it sad? In a moment of inspiration of which Sophia and Betty's hero and heroine fictional detectives would be proud, the girls had decided to visit Ferntower House during 1944. That was the place and time at which, their research had informed them, several reports of sightings of the White Lady had been made by Polish Allied Soldiers who were stationed at Ferntower House during World War 2. Sophia and Betty thought that if they could see the White Lady themselves, or if they could hear first-hand the soldiers' reports, then they could work out the age of the ghostly figure. If they knew the Lady's age, then they could decide exactly when during the nineteenth century to visit, to really discover why she perpetually haunted the hotel.

As Sophia, Betty and Toby made their way towards the old Ferntower House, they could see that it had once been grand indeed. They marvelled that anyone could be rich enough to live in a house that size, not to mention one with a tower (presumably after which the building had been named), that was crowned with crenellations, just like those which were more ordinarily found on the battlements of actual castles!

By 1944, though, it was clear that the house had started to fall into disrepair. There were no rich curtains at the windows. No delicate chandeliers could be glanced through the windows, which were themselves dirty and encrusted with the dust gathered over many, many months, if not years, of neglect. The gardens, once clearly intricately planned and laid out, and no doubt weeded and cared for by a small army of gardening staff, were overgrown and unkempt. Even Sophia and Betty, who didn't have time in their busy lives for gardening themselves (no matter how often both their mothers and fathers tried to encourage them to help with the weeding) could see that the land was growing wild. They recognised dandelions, thistles, nettles, foxgloves, brambles and bindweed, all creeping unrelentingly. The weeds were enveloping and taking over what must have once been neatly tended flower beds and lawns, and choking out the more delicate flowers, herbs and vegetables which had once thrived in both the formal and kitchen gardens.

Sophia and Betty were saddened to see the effect that the passage of time and the lack of care were having on the now-faded Ferntower House. "Although Sophs", said Betty insightfully. "It is 1944. There has been a world war on for several years now, so I'm sure that gardening and looking after posh old houses isn't actually anyone's priority."

Sophia understood that Betty was right, and the realisation focussed her mind even more on the task that lay ahead. The girls might be on a thrilling time-travel adventure, but in the here and now of 1944, and in the world of the Polish soldiers that they hoped to shortly encounter, people's homes, lives, livelihoods, families and loved ones had been shattered, by year after year after year of gruelling fighting, suffering, pain and loss.

With that sobering thought in mind, Sophia determined to make sure that she, Betty and Tobes kept themselves hidden in the shadows during their Ferntower House investigation. She wanted to make sure that they remained sensitive and considerate to the fact that nobody else at Ferntower House that night would have the luxury of jetting back off to the future of a happy family holiday at a spectacular 4-star country holiday resort.

By the light of a big, bright moon on an otherwise dark and humid night, the girls and the trusty Tobes made their unwieldy way, quietly and carefully, to a door that they could just about see, tucked away down the right hand side and towards the rear of the once-great house. ('Probably an old service entrance', Sophia thought.) Sophia and Betty were so intent on keeping to the shadows, almost holding their breath and treading as lightly as they could so that they made as little noise as possible, that they simply didn't notice the spectral, ghostly white figure that silently passed them by as they drew closer to the house. And, if they had been looking, Sophia and Betty would have seen that the fur along Toby's spine was standing fiercely up on end. If he hadn't been so well trained and so attuned to his beloved mistress' mood, and therefore to her current, clear desire for the little party to remain silent and hidden, there's no doubt that Toby would have growled and pulled at his lead to alert his precious girls to the ethereal presence that he could sense, albeit he could not see.

Chapter 14

Having approached what Sophia thought must have been an old service entrance hidden away towards the back of the now quite sad-looking and rather deteriorated Ferntower House, Sophia and Betty pushed gently on the big, old, heavy, wooden door. They were pleasantly surprised to find that it swung open easily, with none of the sinister creaking and cracking which they had thought might ensue, and might disclose their presence.

The girls found themselves in a deserted and very sparsely decorated corridor, which appeared to lead towards the kitchens and the service quarters one way, towards the rear of the house; and to a more opulent, if now faded-looking, hallway and staircase towards the front.

"What do you think, Bets?" asked Sophia. "Which way should we go?"

"Well," said Betty, with an air of authority and confidence that she didn't necessarily feel at that exact moment, "I reckon that the chances of us actually coming across a haunting on the exact date, time and location that we happened to have arrived at Ferntower House are probably pretty slim. However, the chances of us listening in to some of the soldiers who have seen the ghost are quite a bit better. I bet the soldiers chatter and natter to each other for hours before they go to sleep when they're stuck in an old, isolated house like this, in the middle of a world war, miles and miles from their homes and families all that way away in Poland. So, I think that we should head towards the staircase, and try to sneak up, unseen and unheard of course, to the soldiers' sleeping quarters."

With a quick grin and an affirmative nod, Sophia parroted exactly what Betty had said to her a few days ago when she had suggested a sensible plan of action: "That definitely sounds to me like the best idea we've got – so yes, let's do just that!"

With Toby padding quietly beside them, with their hands locked tightly together and with the PT machine knocking gently (and actually quite reassuringly) against Sophia's thigh, Sophia and Betty made their way along the empty corridor and out into the large and lofty hallway. From there, and with the utmost caution and lightness of foot, the brave amateur sleuths and their dedicated and dependable dog, tiptoed together up, up and upwards again, up several winding flights of stairs, until they found themselves standing outside what was clearly the billeted soldiers' dorm room.

"We're here!" whispered Betty triumphantly.

"Yes, but we're also very exposed" worried Sophia. "If one of the soldiers decides to leave the room to use the bathroom or anything, or if anyone else comes up to the stairs to go into the dorm or on their way elsewhere within the house, we'll be seen. We simply can't let that happen Bets, can we?"

Sophia was, quite rightly, very concerned that the sight of two small girls and their dog from the future, visiting 1944 via a time-machine while enjoying a luxury family holiday in Scotland, would be very shocking and upsetting for the soldiers. Plus, she and Betty had seen the 1985 film 'Back to the Future'[4], which explained the time-traveller's paradox: that any action taken by a time-traveller in the past could cause untold ripple effects which could affect the

---

4   *A Steven Spielberg film. Written by Robert Zemeckis and Bob Gale, directed by Zemeckis.*

future (and the real, life here and now of home and of Crieff Hydro Hotel). The film had demonstrated that the ripple effects could be dangerous, potentially even resulting in the purpose for time-travelling, or even the time-traveller him- or herself, ceasing to exist!

Looking around the empty, bare landing on which the girls found themselves, though, it appeared that there was simply nowhere to hide. Certainly nowhere that would be within hearing distance of the soldiers' dorm.

Aggghhhh!!! What on earth should Sophia and Betty do?!

Chapter 15

Sophia, Betty and Toby were standing, in the middle of a dark night in 1944, outside the Polish soliders' dorm room in Ferntower House on a completely empty, unfurnished landing. The landing was lit only by the sliver of moonlight which poured softly through a small window in the wall of the staircase they had just climbed. The girls had been horrified to find that there was nowhere for them to hide within hearing distance of the soldiers' sleeping quarters, and they were terrified by the prospect that they could be spotted by one of the soldiers at any moment. At the same time, however, they were appalled at the thought that they had come so far towards, and were now so close to, solving the mystery of Crieff Hydro's White Lady ghost, but may have to consider aborting the mission after all. For several moments the girls simply stood still, unsure what to do or even think next. They were paralysed into inaction by indecision and doubt.

"Oh no, Sophs," moaned Betty after just another minute. "I've just realised something that makes things even worse!"

"Even worse?!" cried Sophia in an anguished whisper. "How could things be even worse?"

"Well," said Betty. "I'm afraid that we didn't factor into our plan the fact that the soldiers billeted here are all from Poland. Even though I bet a lot of them will understand and speak English, I'm sure they'll all just chat to each other in Polish when there's no one else around. Even if we could find somewhere to hide and try to hear about their encounters with the White Lady, we wouldn't understand what they were saying! Neither of us is fluent in Polish!"

"Oh, you're right!" gasped Sophia, immediately grasping the enormity of the flaw in their otherwise perfect plan. "Oh no, does that mean that we should just abandon this investigation after all? That would be *such* a shame, though, especially because we don't really have any other ideas as to how to find out more about Crieff Hydro's ghost."

Before Betty had the chance to reply, however, the difficult and unwelcome decision was entirely taken out of Sophia's and Betty's hands. Without warning, the dorm room door was suddenly and quickly pushed open, and Sophia and Betty found themselves face-to-face with a big, strong and slightly scary-looking real life Polish World War 2 soldier, who appeared to be making his way towards the bathroom.

Even if the soldier had needed to use the bathroom, however, he immediately stopped dead in his tracks at the completely unexpected, completely *inexplicable*, sight of two young girls, clearly healthier, wealthier and better-fed than any children he had seen since long before the war had begun. One of the girls was wearing denim shorts, which he had never seen on a girl, and the other was wearing sporty clothes made out of some sort of stretchy, shiny material, the like of which he had never seen before. There was also a dog and a strange-looking clock-type machine, and all were bound together with leads and belts. The girls were holding hands and staring up at him in shock!

Sophia, Betty and Toby froze. They didn't know what to think, what to say, how to react. They didn't know whether to be frightened and run away and use the PT machine to return to the safety of the real life here and now at the hotel; or whether to stay, risk the ripple effect, and maybe have one last chance of learning about the Polish soldiers' experiences of the White Lady hauntings after all.

Again, though, for the second time in very quick succession, the decision was taken for them. The hitherto somewhat scary-looking soldier burst into a great big grin and said, in English but with a strong Polish accent and with friendly laughter in his eyes, "Well, what on earth do we have here then?! Where have you lot come from and how in heaven have you ended up here?!"

Before Sophia or Betty could gather their thoughts and even begin to explain, the soldier even joked: "You all look like you've come from another world, another life – and a better one at that! You haven't landed here from the future have you, to tell us to keep going, to keep fighting, and that we're going to win this flippin' frightful war?!"

Sophia and Betty looked at each other incredulously, and then broke into beaming grins themselves!

"Well, erm, yes, actually!" laughed the girls in unison. Then, the next minute, the girls' laughter redoubled at the look of utter shock and disbelief on the young soldier's face. That quickly gave way to a look of wonder, happiness and hope, when it dawned on him that his words, said in jest, actually, genuinely, were true!

"What?! You're kidding?! Unbelieveable!" cried the soldier. "Well, I no longer need to visit the bathroom, that's for sure. What I need now is to have a good long chat with you girls and to introduce you to my friends. Come on, come with me, it seems like you've got some very exciting explaining to do!"

As the soldier turned back to the door of the dorm room, Toby jumped up and nuzzled against him happily. It was as if the defensive but perceptive pooch had sussed out the soldier and realised that he was a friend, and certainly no threat to Toby's dear mistress and Betty. "Oh, ok, and you too, Boss!" chuckled the soldier. He tickled Toby on his favourite spot behind his ears, and referred to him by the same affectionate nickname that the soldier called his own beloved dog, whom he missed so much while he was so far away from home.

"We'd be very happy to talk to you and your friends about why were are here" said Betty to the soldier.

"Yes," agreed Sophia, "because there's something that we'd like you to explain to us too!"

Chapter 16

After Sophia, Betty and Toby had been properly introduced to the nice young solider, Piotr (pronounced 'Peter'), and to his group of friends, the shocked and stunned soldiers gathered around to hear what the strange little girls, who had magically appeared before them, had to say.

Still holding tight to each other and remaining tethered to Toby and the PT machine, Sophia and Betty explained that the PT machine was, in fact, an actual, working time- and place- travel machine, which had allowed Sophia and Betty to investigate, and even solve, several real life mysteries from throughout history. Bit by bit the soldiers' disbelief dissipated, and gave way to awe, admiration and delight, as they understood just how amazing the PT machine was; how brave and exuberant Sophia and Betty were; and, most of all, how fantastically brilliant it was for them to learn that the war was nearly over, that the Allies would win, and that life would be prosperous and happy for millions and millions of people in the future all because of the sacrifices that they and their comrades were making in the fight against prejudice and persecution.

"We have arrived here at Ferntower House tonight" went on Sophia, "because we are currently trying to solve the mystery of Crieff Hydro's White Lady ghost. We learned about the ghost when we were reading about the hotel on the way up to our holiday there, and our research told us that Polish soldiers stationed at Ferntower House during the second world war had reported sightings of the ghost."

"Yes," continued Betty "and we thought that if we could learn more about the hauntings from you, then we would be able to move forward with our mystery-solving mission."

"We would love to hear anything that you can tell us about the White Lady" said Sophia to the soldiers "but one thing in particular that we would really like to know, is how old do you think she is?"

"If we know that," explained Betty "we will know approximately which date during the nineteenth century to visit with the PT machine, so as to find out the real story of the Crieff Hydro White Lady once and for all!"

"Well," murmured a soldier named Aleksander, whose face had gone pale at the mere mention of the ghost. "I think I can help you out. I was just starting to tell the boys here, before Piotr burst back into the room with you, that I s-s-saw the W-w-hite Lady – I'm absolutely certain that I did – j-just, just last night."

The room fell silent. It suddenly felt as though everyone in it was holding his or her breath, as Aleksander gulped deeply, and steeled himself for relaying his ghostly encounter.

"We had quite a gruelling day of training exercises yesterday, and I was exhausted. To be honest, I've also been feeling a little bit down over the last week or so. It has felt like this war is never-ending. Although the people of Crieff have been kind and welcoming while we have been stationed here at Ferntower House, I have been feeling homesick and very much missing my parents and my grandparents back home. All in all, I just wanted some time to myself, to think and walk and take some comfort from this beautiful landscape. At least there is peace here now, even if there is war everywhere else."

At this, the other soldiers nodded gently, all of them completely understanding how Aleksander had felt.

"So, after rations, I went, by myself, down to Lady Mary's Walk. Usually, if I walk along by the river for an hour or so, I feel much better, refreshed even, and ready to face another day, another week, another month of exercises and of fighting. L-last n-night, though," Aleksander's face appeared to drain itself of colour once again, "last n-night I felt the s-strangest, s-strangest feeling..."

After a short pause and a deep breath, Aleksander carried on. "It was like all of the warmth of the late spring evening had been spirited away all of a sudden. A freezing cold chill crept over me and I even felt a short, sharp, stabbing sensation, right here in the centre of my chest. I turned my head, this way and that, to try to see what might be making feel so cold, so shivery, and... and th-th-that's when I saw it, when I saw her!"

Aleksander's face was flushed now. He was staring off into an empty corner of the room, as if he was re-living and re-seeing the moment that he encountered the ghost.

"Sh-she was white, all white, from her head to the hem of her floor-length, old-fashioned gown. She was gliding, floating even, along the path down at

Lady Mary's Walk. She was travelling in the same direction as me, and I had the queerest idea that she had come from behind where I was standing and had passed right through me, as if I wasn't there, before carrying on her walk up ahead. I felt shocked and bewildered, and I have felt frightened every time I have thought about it since. But, looking back now, I realise that I didn't actually feel frightened at the time. Cold, startled and shaken, certainly, but I don't actually think that there was any harm or malice in the White Lady. No, no, I had no sense of horror or fear of her at the time."

As Aleksander paused in the telling of his story once again, this time it was Sophia and Betty who were nodding, and excitedly! Alexander's account tallied almost exactly with their own experience of what they had thought was the White Lady in the Victorian Baths. The two amateur sleuths were thrilled! This was corroborating evidence – the gold dust of the detective world!

Never one to be distracted from the task at hand, however, Sophia questioned her witness, Aleksander, carefully. She didn't want to disturb his reverie, but she wanted to ensure that they got as much valuable information out of him as they could.

"That's amazing to hear, Aleksander, thank you so much for telling us what you saw and how you felt. There's just one more crucial piece of information that we are after, though: when you looked at the White Lady ahead of you, did she turn around at all? Did you get to see her face, and do you think you could you make out her age?"

"Oh yes," said Aleksander, smiling now that the initial shock of recounting his encounter had passed. "The White Lady turned and looked right at me. She stared me straight and strong in the face, almost as if she was trying to see who I was, perhaps even to see whether she recognised me. She didn't, of course, and she soon turned back away from me as if to carry on her walk. At that point, she disappeared – she simply vanished into the twilight. I lingered for a minute or two, to gather myself and to catch my breath. I actually think that I had been too stunned to breathe for pretty much most of the encounter. Then I ran back up to Ferntower House and jumped right into bed before anyone could see what kind of state I was in."

"But, but," shouted Betty, unable to contain her curiosity for a second longer, "how old was she? Do you know how old she was?"

"Oh, oh yes, sorry!" said Aleksander sheepishly. "She was a young woman – a very beautiful young woman, actually – of around 18 or 19 years old, I'd say."

"Yes!" whooped Sophia and Betty joyfully! "We've got it! We've got the info we need to now actually visit the White Lady, back when she was alive and a beautiful young woman! Surely, from there, we can finally solve this ghostly history's mystery!"

Chapter 17

Sophia, Betty and Tobes said a fond farewell to the friendly soldiers that they had met at Ferntower House in 1944. The soldiers had been delighted to see them – what an astonishing interlude in their otherwise difficult and draining wartime life?! The soldiers thanked the girls keenly for sharing their knowledge from the future that the continued war effort was worthwhile and would succeed. In turn, the girls gave the soldiers their heartfelt thanks for the incredible lengths to which they were going to ensure safety and security for future generations. Then, before there was a risk of the girls' time-travelling interference with the past having any detrimental effect upon the future, Sophia turned the time period hands of the amazing PT machine back to the real life present day.

Whooshkazzamflashzingwow!!!, In an instant, the girls and a very dizzy Toby arrived, safely and happily, back to Crieff Hydro's golf course in the late spring of 2021.

Of course, in the real life here and now, not a minute had passed since Sophia, Betty and Tobes had departed for 1944, even though the girls knew that they had actually been visiting Ferntower House and its grounds for several hours. So, acting as if nothing at all unusual had happened, the girls simply followed the last few golfers off the green and into the warmth, comfort and jollity of another holiday evening at the Hydro. It wasn't very long afterwards, though, that the exhausted but exhilarated little girls were surprising Sophia's mum and dad with a request, for once, for a nice, early night.

The next morning, while enjoying an even more mountainous breakfast than they had yet had to date, Sophia and Betty chatted to Sophia's mum, dad and little brother Ted about what they would do with their precious last day and a half of their fun-filled stay at Crieff Hydro. On the girls' definite 'still to do' list were one more pony ride, a fun family tennis session and a last blast around Action Glen. That would include an air rifle lesson, a high wire treetop adventure session and a final tear around with Ted at Glen's Adventure Park. Other than that, Sophia and Betty said, they just wanted to make sure that they had time for one more lovely long walk with Tobes around the woodland and grounds surrounding the hotel.

Feeling relaxed, rested and pleased that all three children and the dog had enjoyed such a superb half term break, Sophia's parents agreed readily that their plans for the last day and a half sounded spot on. As Ted was due to enjoy one last play session at Big Country with his holiday buddies that morning, Sophia's mum suggested that it might make sense for Sophia and Betty to take Toby and go off for a couple of hours by themselves straight away. The family could all meet up again in the Hub at midday, in time for a quick drink and a light snack, before they headed over to Action Glen together that afternoon.

Sophia and Betty exchanged an excited glance and a secret grin between themselves. This was it! It was now or never! This was the one and only chance that they would get to finally discover the real story behind the spectre that was Crieff Hydro's White Lady.

As soon as Sophia, Betty and Toby were alone once again, the girls grabbed their go-bags and hiked, as fast as they could, to the lovely Lady Mary's

Walk. Knowing, as they did, that it was a favourite spot of Lady Mary Murray's, and after hearing that Aleksander had experienced such a clear and close encounter with the White Lady there, they both felt sure that it would be just the place to carry out this most crucial stage of their investigation.

When they arrived at Lady Mary's Walk, the girls were pleased to discover that the riverside trail was completely deserted. It seemed that all of the other happy holiday-makers at Crieff Hydro Hotel were taking the opportunity to make the most of all the entertainments on site, as the half term holiday week began to draw to a close. Sophia, Betty and Tobes appeared to have the whole area to themselves. Perfect!

"Right then Sophs," said Betty. "We know that the White Lady is the ghost of a pretty young woman, aged about 18 or 19. We also know that she was old enough to have a favourite walk by around 1815 and she that she lived until 1886. She was wealthy and privileged and, to reach 1886, she must have lived until a ripe old age – I'd say we should guess around 90."

"Yes," said Sophia thoughtfully, picking up and

running with Betty's line of thinking. "So, if she was around 90 in 1886, then she will have been born around 1796 and she will have been 18 years old in..."

"1814!" calculated Betty quickly. "Let's set the PT machine to early in 1814 and see exactly what we can learn about Lady Mary Murry from that time."

"Yes, let's" agreed Sophia. She didn't want to lose another minute before really embarking upon another history mystery. "Ok, I've got Toby on the lead and I've got the PT machine just here. Come and grab my hand, let's move the history hand to 1814, and ..."

W h o o s h k a z z a m f l a s h z i n g w o w !!! Before the girls even knew it, they had time-travelled back to early 1814. They were now in exactly the same spot in which they had been standing just one second earlier in 2021, but they had been transported, in the blink of an eye, backwards through two hundred and seven years!

Chapter 18

Were it not for the facts that the girls had felt the now-familiar jolt, thwack and flash sensation of time-travelling via the PT machine; that it was now the cold, damp and drizzly grey of a Scottish January day; and that some of the trees and bushes that lined the picturesque path and bordered the banks of the beautiful River Earn were much less mature, and therefore much smaller, than they had been just a moment earlier, there was nothing to betray that the girls had gone anywhere (or, indeed, any-when!) at all. Sophia and Betty were delighted to note that Lady Mary's Walk looked exactly the same in 1814 as it did in 2021, and that this very special place had remained intact, in all of its natural beauty, despite the passage, in reality, of over two hundred years.

However, the girls were not at Lady Mary's Walk on a jaunt to enjoy the scenery. Oh no! They were on essential history mystery-solving business, and so it was only a matter of minutes before Sophia and Betty were concentrating on the plan at hand, rather than on the untouched beauty of their surroundings.

"So Betty, now that we're here, what do you

suggest?" asked Sophia.

Betty looked at Sophia intently – she was deep in thought. After a minute or so, she answered. "I'm afraid I honestly don't think we've got enough to go on to do very much more than wander up and down Lady Mary's Walk for a while. I think that we just have to hope beyond hope that we have landed here on a day when Lady Mary Murray also decides to take a turn on her favourite trail."

"Yes, I suppose you're right" said Sophia. "I do think we've managed to learn as much about Lady Mary as we could from the internet, and I think that trying to visit the time when we've calculated she would be a young woman is a sensible approach, but I agree that other than hoping for a chance encounter with her here today, there's not much else that we can really do. I think that it's just a matter of 'fingers crossed'..."

With that, Sophia, Betty and Toby resigned themselves to just enjoying the walk. That was actually easier said than done, for the girls anyway, as they were dressed in shorts and t-shirts, which were completely comfortable on a warm and sunny late spring day in May 2021, but which were absolutely inappropriate and out of place on a cold, wet morning in January 1814. They walked quickly and quietly, hugging their arms around themselves and shuddering – partly with the cold and partly with the hopeful anticipation of gaining a lucky break in the 'case'.

And just then, without warning and in an unbelievably lucky twist of fate for our indefatigable historical investigators, there she was! Yes, yes! It really was her – it *must* be! The real life, stunningly beautiful, young Lady Mary Murray was there, right there, just a few steps ahead of Sophia and Betty! The two girls stopped in their tracks and stood, stock still. They stared, entranced, at the elegant young lady before them.

Lady Mary Murray, aged around eighteen, was slowly meandering along the newly-laid, charmingly pretty, river walk. She was very richly and cosily attired in a heavy, velvet, multi-layered, floor-length dress and a fur-lined frock-coat. She was also wearing tall, black, buttoned-up leather boots and a ruffled velvet and woollen winter bonnet. Her hands were tucked deep into a fluffy, furry cylindrical hand-warmer which Sophia knew was known as a muff. She was the absolute picture of nineteenth century classic country style, and exuded comfort, luxury and warmth. Sophia and Betty felt both awe-struck and a little envious as they stood, shivering, in their somewhat skimpy and totally insufficient modern-day spring cotton clothes.

As Sophia and Betty stopped dead, so too did Toby, attuned (as he always was) to Sophia's feelings and to exactly what she needed from him. Both girls knew that it was absolutely essential that Lady Mary Murray did not see them. This was one mystery from history where, despite their research and knowledge from the real life present day, they actually knew very little indeed about the life and the experiences of the historical protagonist (here, Lady Mary Murray). If Sophia and Betty allowed themselves to impinge on Lady Murray's life at all, in any way, the results could be significant indeed. The consequences would be completely unknown and could be harmful, indefinite and potentially even devastating for Lady Murray, for other people with whom she came into contact throughout her life, and even for descendants for years and years to come.

In an unspoken unity, the girls and Toby knew that they had to remain absolutely silent and absolutely still until they could be sure that Lady Mary Murray's back was turned completely to them. At that point, they could try to make a soundless dive into the undergrowth at the edge of the woodland that bordered the riverside path.

Suddenly the moment came. Both girls realised, at the exact same instant, that Lady Mary had stopped walking, her back was fully turned and... it was go time! Feeling glad now that they were only wearing light and comfy clothes that allowed them to move freely, quickly and noiselessly, Sophia and Betty, along with Toby on a short, tight lead, leapt with all their might but as light-footedly as ever they could, into the cover of the dense and shaded woods. The girls were very pleased indeed to note that the trees which surrounded them at just this point along Lady Mary's Walk were tall, closely packed evergreen firs, which provided strong, dark and downy cover, and obscured the little party from sight. What's more, the deep, soft, gently browning pine needles which blanketed the woodland floor muffled any noise so effectively that Sophia and Betty were able to finally let out the breath that they realised they had both been holding, and to silently rejoice that they had made it to cover without incident.

And that was it – the girls were on a real life stakeout! This was, of course, something for which Sophia and Betty, as enthusiastic amateur sleuths, had prepared and rehearsed many times back in their home village in 2021. Unable to believe their luck at finally being able to put all their hours of shadowing and reconnaissance work into practice, the girls moved stealthily into a position from which they would be able to watch their target, and even to hear anything she might have to say if she were to speak at all.

Aware, as any good detective would be, that stakeouts can take time and patience, the girls sat down and made themselves comfortable on the bouncy, cushion-like ground, deeply covered as it was in fallen pine needles. Toby, of course, took the opportunity to snuggle up in Sophia's lap and all three watched and waited, and then watched and waited some more, to see what would happen next.

Chapter 19

Sophia Slewfoot, her best friend Betty Babbington, and her faithful Beagle Toby were coming towards the end of their fantastic half term holiday at Crieff Hydro Hotel at the gateway to the beautiful Scottish Highlands. Before their holiday came to an end they had some last minute, fun-filled activities to enjoy. Oh, and of course, they had a history's mystery ghost story to solve: the mystery of Criff Hydro's White Lady.

It was in the process of doing the latter that the girls now found themselves on a real life stake-out, on a January day on Lady Mary's Walk on the Crieff estate, back in the year 1814. The girls were watching Lady Mary Murray, whom they suspected of being Crieff Hydro's ghost, as she dawdled on what the girls' research had informed them was her most beloved of all the woodland and country trails within this rugged but spectacular landscape.

Lady Murray had actually stopped walking a short time ago. It now appeared, from where the girls were watching, from their hidden woodland lookout, that Lady Murray was waiting for someone. Rather than continuing to amble along the path, the young lady had started to pace up and down only a very small section of the trail, and she kept glancing at her watch.

After fifteen minutes or so, the person for whom Lady Mary Murray had obviously been waiting appeared. It was a man, a much older man, who looked to be in his late forties or early fifties. He was very grandly dressed indeed, with a formal-looking suit with tails and waistcoat, in a quite ornate and flamboyant eighteenth century 'Regency' style. He wore a stiff, high necked collar and cravat, and a flowing, calf-length, velvet-lined, tweed overcoat. He also wore a black, felt, top hat and had greying, curling hair, a bushy beard and large moustache. The man also had huge furry sideburns, which looked, in this weather, to be keeping his ageing but friendly face nice and warm, almost like a home-grown, soft and snuggly snood!

"Nathaniel! Oh, Nathaniel! I'm so glad you came!" cried Lady Mary happily, as she threw her arms around the older man's neck. "I haven't seen you in an age! I've missed you these last few weeks, I've missed you so much!"

"My darling Mary," began the man. "I am so, so happy to see you, and I have missed you terribly too, but I am afraid I come bearing some sad, well, some awful news." The man's face, friendly and warm as it was, fell when he saw the confusion and sadness that his words brought to the lovely young lady's bright, blue eyes.

"Some awful news? Oh dear. Are you ill? Is something wrong? Oh my love, whatever it is I am sure that we can face it together! Surely it won't be long now until we can be married, and I can be your wife, and then we can meet any challenges that life throws our way, together?!" The young Lady Mary was clearly very much in love with this older gentleman and was hoping to be married to him soon. She seemed not to want to put too much stock in what he was saying about being the bearer of bad news.

Sophia and Betty looked at each other with raised eyebrows. This was unexpected. They hadn't known that Lady Mary Murray had been in love with an older man. As far as they knew from their research, she had married someone else, a man named James Bonar of Kimmerghame. He had been born in 1795 and would have been much closer in age to Lady Mary. Was something about to go wrong in the love story between the lady and this older man, Nathaniel, that would cause her to be unhappy? Might that explain why she would return, after her death, to haunt this spot and others around Crieff for evermore?

"My dear Mary", said the man. "Although I love you more than life itself and although it was my greatest wish in the world to be married to you so that we may spend the rest of our lives together, alas it is not to be. You will remember that, before I met you, I was engaged to another lady. Well, I am afraid that she has sued me in the law courts for breaking my promise of marriage to her. The courts have ruled against me and declared that I must pay a huge fine. Most devastatingly, though, I am eternally sorry to say, the courts have ordered that I must adhere to my original promise and marry her anyway. I am being forced to marry her even though I know, and she knows, that we are not at all in love. The other lady is jealous that I have found true love with you and she has her heart set on my money and my estate. Unfortunately, the law of the land favours the promise of an old engagement over the currency of our true love now, and so there is nothing, nothing at all, that I can do about it. The fact is, my love, that after our meeting today, I can never see you again. Not unless we bump into each other in society somewhere. Even then we shall have to see each other only as strangers, not as friends, and certainly never again as lovers. I am sorry, my love, to break your heart as well as my own." At this, the man turned away from Lady Mary, broke down, and wept.

Lady Mary Murray looked stunned. For several moments she stood, her face blank, as if she were simply unable to process or accept what Nathaniel was telling her. Then, with a deep breath, and a look of dignified resignation mixed with deep sadness, Lady Mary said "Mr Gow, it has been a pleasure getting to know you. These past few months of corresponding and meeting with you, of walking with you here in this most special of places, and of dancing with you to your wonderful musical compositions both at Ferntower House and at society gatherings in Edinburgh and elsewhere, have been the happiest of my life. However, I understand the predicament that you are in and I do not wish to make things harder for you, nor more heart-breaking for myself. So, I will leave you now, with my sincere good wishes for the future. I hope that we may both eventually find happiness elsewhere, however unlikely that may seem in this moment. Goodbye, my lov..., erm, Mr Gow, goodbye." And with that, Lady Murray turned to leave.

Sophia and Betty were wide-eyed with surprise, sadness and a slight sense of mortification at the moving and very private scene that they had just witnessed. They felt incredibly sorry for Lady Mary and for Nathaniel Gow, who had obviously been head over heels in love with each other, but who could now never be together again. They also felt full of admiration for Lady Mary, who was clearly struggling with her emotions, but who was behaving in a self-respecting and kind manner, so that she did not make things even more difficult than they obviously already were.

Just as Lady Mary was about to hurry away, no doubt to the solace of her home and family, Mr Gow called her back. "Thank you Lady Mary, for our precious few months together and for being so strong and so understanding today. I just want you to know that, as a lasting memento of our love, I have composed a song for you. I have left the sheet music with your father and I will make sure that it is played in dance halls and ballrooms throughout the land for years and years to come. Every time you hear the tune, I hope that you will remember our happy times together."

Lady Mary and Mr Gow then smiled sadly at each other for one last time, and each turned and went their separate ways.

As soon as Lady Mary's Walk was completely quiet and empty once again, Sophia, Betty and Toby roused themselves from their hidden woodland lookout, stepped out into the open air of the riverside path, and dusted off the bracken and pine needles that had clung to their cotton clothes. Both girls felt a strange mixture of, on the one hand, satisfaction at having almost certainly solved the history's mystery which they had set out to do and, on the other, a sense of real melancholy at having witnessed the sorrowful end of a genuine romantic tragedy. Quietly, in tacit agreement that they should get back to the safety, comfort and happiness of their real life here and now Crieff Hydro holiday, the girls held on to each other and to Toby tightly and slowly set the hands of the PT machine back to the present date and time.

For what they knew would be the final time this half term, the girls and Toby experienced a last w h o o s h k a z z a m f l a s h z i n g w o w !!!, and found themselves, still on Lady Mary's Walk, but back on a warm, sunny, spring morning in May 2021.

Chapter 20

"Sophs," said Betty, as she turned her face to the warm, bright sunshine that was bouncing off the rippling River Earn and dappling through the now-huge trees and bushes that lined Lady Mary's Walk, "I feel really quite flat after seeing how Lady Mary and Nathanial Gow were forced to break up their relationship like that."

"Me too, Bets" agreed Sophia, "but I do know just what we need, to really lift our spirits...!"

"Oh yes!" cried Betty, brightening at once. "Let's get back to the hotel and get stuck into all of our remaining activities!"

"Exactly!" laughed Sophia and, before they even made it back to the Hub where they were meeting Sophia's family for a quick drink and a bite, the two best friends were chatting and giggling again, in happy anticipation of a fun-filled afternoon.

And fun-filled it was too! After some initial hesitation and trepidation on Sophia's part (although never on Betty's or Ted's), the family enjoyed an unbelievably exhilarating zip wire extravaganza at Crieff Hydro's Treetop Adventure experience. A little while later, to their mother's slight consternation, Sophia and Ted both discovered that they were an excellent shot with an air rifle. "Good coordination, probably from all that tennis!" said Sophia's dad proudly, as her mum rolled her eyes and muttered "Hmm, money well-spent then!" The family then had a final race around Glen's Adventure Park, bouncing, wheeling, sliding, climbing, snacking and laughing until, finally, they were all absolutely well and truly tired out.

In fact, such was the toll taken on Sophia and Betty after their time-travelling adventure and surprisingly saddening stake-out that morning, and after their hugely entertaining but physically exhausting afternoon, that the girls felt reluctantly obliged to pull out of their final, early evening, pony hack.

It was a shame that they did, however. The hack had been due to traverse the golf course – the site of the old Ferntower House. Had the girls proceeded with their twilight pony ride they would have seen, had they thought to look, a ghostly white figure in a flowing Regency gown, swaying, whirling and twirling across the soft, green grass of the immaculately kept course, as if to a pretty dancing tune that only she could hear. The glowing spectre, had anyone been able to see, had her beautiful long-lashed eyes closed and wore a wistful, dream-like smile on her face. She looked, for all the world, as if she were re-living, for evermore, the happiest time of her life.

Back at Crieff Hydro Hotel itself, Sophia, Betty and Sophia's family had a final hearty and delicious meal at the Terrace before retiring to their rooms to pack up their belongings and to get in an early night as their holiday came nearly to its end. There would just be one more momentous breakfast and (if they could manage it!) a family turn on the tennis courts the next morning, before the happy holiday party would head back down, south of the border, to their Cheshire home.

In their room, Sophia and Betty pulled out their notebooks and tablet and chatted briefly about what they had discovered over the last few days. When they consulted the notes of their earlier research and did a little more reading-up on the internet about Mr Nathaniel Gow, they learned that it was indeed true that the man had been forced by the law courts, in 1814, to marry a lady following an earlier broken engagement. It was also true that Mr Gow, a famous composer, musician and society man in the late eighteenth and early nineteenth centuries, had known Lady Mary Murray (he had met her through being a friend of her father) and had written a tune in her name. They already knew that, some years after that, Lady Mary Murray had gone on to marry another man, and that she lived for many years into the late nineteenth century. They therefore agreed that she must, at last, have found some happiness in her life, so that her story did not necessarily seem have to have a completely unhappy ending after all. Sophia and Betty felt sure, though, from what they had learned from their research, from talking to the Polish soldiers at Ferntower House in 1944, and from what they had seen and heard first-hand on Lady Mary's Walk in 1814, that Lady Mary Murray must indeed be Crieff Hydro's White Lady ghost.

Using their powers of reasoning and their detective's instinct, the two girls decided that the White Lady was most definitely not an evil, malevolent or a discontented ghost. Rather, she was a happy spirit, who chose, in death, to re-live, for all eternity, the years at Crieff in which she had been young, beautiful and the most happy and hopeful in life.

It was nice to know, thought the girls, as they drifted off into a much-needed deep and restful last night's sleep, that Crieff Hydro had been a joyful place for Lady Mary Murray, for the soldiers who made it their home-from-home during the war, for Sophia and Betty and Sophia's family, and for so many other hundreds and hundreds of families and friends who had found welcome, shelter, health and happiness there, throughout the estate's long, proud, fascinating and enduring history.

✳ ✳ ✳

Epilogue

The reader should note that, while internet research* does suggest that it is true that Mr Nathaniel Gow was a famous composer, musician and society man in Scotland in the late eighteenth and early nineteenth centuries; that he had potentially known Lady Mary Murray; that he had written a tune seemingly in her name; and that he had been forced by the law courts to marry a lady following an earlier broken engagement, the characters created and the story told in this Sophia Slewfoot Special Edition are entirely fictional. No assertion of any kind is made or intended in relation to any person (alive now or throughout history) or any event. Apart from covering off any potential legal implications, that does mean, of course, that, in real life, the mystery of the Crieff Hydro White Lady still remains ripe for resolving...!

These are the websites that Sophia and Betty consulted as part of their research when investigating this Crieff Hydro history's mystery:

- https://www.crieffhydro.com
- https://perthshirecrieffstrathearnlocalhistor. blogspot.com/2012/07/story-of-ferntower-house. html
- https://tunearch.org/wiki/Annotation:Lady_Mary_ Murray
- https://tunearch.org/wiki/Biography:Nathaniel_ Gow
- https://www.regencydances.org/paper022.php

✻ ✻ ✻

If you have enjoyed this book, please visit **www.sophiaslewfoot.co.uk** to find out more!

From the website you can sign up to receive news and notifications of forthcoming Sophia Slewfoot Solves History's Mysteries books and you can follow Sophia Slewfoot on social media (Twitter @SSlewfoot; Instagram sophiaslewfoot).

History fan Sophia Slewfoot is a budding amateur detective who loves nothing more than curling up with a good whodunnit or, even better, finding a real life mystery to unravel. Join Sophia, her best friend Betty and her beloved Beagle Toby, as they embark on amazing adventures to solve some of the many mysteries which, throughout history and even to this day, have otherwise remained unexplained...

The Ghost Ship Mary Celeste

What happened to the Victorian ghost ship, the Mary Celeste? Was it magic or malevolence of some kind which caused the crew to disappear? Can Sophia solve the mystery that has baffled some of the world's greatest minds over the last century? Can she somehow even save the day?!

Delve into myth, legend, fact and more than a little fiction, to accompany Sophia on the very first of her history's mystery-solving missions.

The Mystery of the Oak Island Treasure

What is the mystery of the Oak Island Treasure? Is it true that pirate treasure lays buried in a pit on the infamous Oak Island, and that a curse follows all who seek it? Can Sophia and Betty solve the mystery that has confounded some of the world's most committed treasure hunters over the last few hundred years? Can they even find (and recover?!) the fabled priceless treasure?!

Delve into myth, legend, fact and more than a little fiction, to accompany Sophia and Betty on a nerve-wracking, nail-biting, history's mystery-solving mission.

Shergar the Stolen Stallion

Sophia and her best friend Betty Babbington have found themselves embroiled in a shocking mystery which combines their love of history with their passion for all things horse riding-related.

What happened to Shergar? How did he disappear, as if into thin air? Can Sophia and Betty solve the mystery that rocked the racing world and baffled the police, international investigators and the world's media? Can they even discover (and rescue?!) the magnificent racing champion?!

Delve into myth, legend, fact and more than a little fiction, to accompany Sophia and Betty on a fast-paced, perilous history's mystery-solving mission.

Sophia Slewfoot Solves
**Crieff Hydro's
White Lady**
History's Mysteries

Marie-Louise Gregory
Illustrated by Nicola Brooks

A CIP catalogue record for this title is available from the
British Library.

ISBN 978-1-7398655-2-8 (Paperback)

2 4 6 8 10 9 7 5 3 1

First published 2022

Muddy Publishing Ltd
www.muddypublishing.com